PILGRIMS' PROJECT

PILGRIMS' PROJECT

Robert F. Young

CHAPTER I

"I'd like to apply for a wife," I said.

The Marriage Administration girl inserted an application blank into the talk-typer on her desk. Her eyes were light blue and her hair was dark brown and she was wearing a Mayflower dress with a starched white collar. "Name and number?"

"Roger Bartlett. 14479201-B."

"Date of birth?"

"January 17, 2122."

"What is your occupation, Mr. Bartlett?"

"Senior Sentry at the Cadillac Cemetery."

She raised her eyes. Her hair was combed tightly back into a chignon and her face looked round and full like a little girl's.

"Oh. Have there been any exhumings recently, Mr. Bartlett?"

"Not at Cadillac," I said.

"I'm glad. I think it's a shame the way the ghouls carry on, don't you? Imagine anyone having the effrontery to rob a sacred car-grave!"

Her voice sounded sincere enough but I got the impression she was ridiculing me—why, I couldn't imagine. She could not know I was lying.

"Someday they'll rob one grave too many," I said flatly, "and earn the privilege of digging their own."

She lowered her eyes—rather abruptly, I thought. "Last place of employment?"

"Ford Acres."

The longer I looked at her, the more she affected me. The little-girl aspect of her face was misleading. There was nothing little-girlish about her lithe body, and her stern, high-bosomed dress could not conceal the burgeoning of full breasts or the breathless sweep of waist and shoulders.

Illogically, she reminded me of a landscape I had seen recently at a clandestine art exhibit. I had wandered into the dim and dismal place more out of boredom than curiosity, and I had hardly gone two steps beyond the cellar door when the painting caught my eye. It was called "Twentieth Century Landscape."

PILGRIMS' PROJECT

In the foreground, a blue river flowed, and beyond the river a flower-flecked meadow spread out to a series of small, forested hills. Beyond the hills a great cumulus formation towered into the sky like an impossibly tall and immaculate mountain. There was only one other object in the scene—the lofty, lonely speck of a soaring bird.

An impossible landscape by twenty-second century standards; an impossible analogy by any standards. And yet that's what I thought of, standing there in Marriage Administration Headquarters, the stone supporting pillars encircling me like the petrified trunks of a decapitated forest and the unwalled departments buzzing with activity.

"Can you give us some idea of the kind of wife you want, Mr. Bartlett?"

I wanted to say that I didn't want any kind of a wife, that the only reason I was applying for one was because I was on the wrong side of twenty-nine and had received my marriage summons in yesterday's mail. But I didn't say anything of the sort. It wasn't wise to question Marriage Administration procedure.

But I didn't take it lying down. Not quite. I said: "The wife I want is a pretty remote item from the one I'll probably get."

"What we want consciously is invariably different from what we want unconsciously, Mr. Bartlett. The Marriage Integrator's true benefit to humanity arises from the fact that it matches marriageable men and women in accordance with their unconscious rather than with their conscious desires. However, any information you may care to impart will be entered on your data card and *might* influence the final decision."

"I don't know," I said.

And I didn't. The celibacy I had endured rather than apply for a wife before reaching the maximum age of twenty-nine had resulted in the total sublimation of my sexual desires. Women had lost reality for me—at least, until this morning.

I looked around the huge chamber in search of inspiration. The various departments were cramped with desks and marriage officials, enlivened here and there by gray- or black-garbed secretaries. The department next to the one in which I stood constituted the headquarters for the Marriage

Enforcement Police and less than ten feet away from me a gaunt MEP captain brooded behind an austere marble desk.

Apparently he had been fasting, for his charcoal gray coat hung loosely on his wide shoulders. His cheeks were cadaverous, his thin lips pale. His thin nose jutted sharply from his narrow face, giving him a bleak, hungry look, and his deep, somber eyes intensified the impression.

Those eyes, I realized suddenly, were gazing directly into mine.

So far as I knew, there was nothing about my appearance to pique the interest of an MEP official. My Roger Williams suit was conventional enough; I had doffed my black, wide-brimmed hat upon entering the building and now held it at my waist in the prescribed manner; I was above average in height, but not noticeably so, and if my yellow hair and gray eyes failed to match the dour decorum of my clothing, I could hardly be held responsible for the defection. Nevertheless, there was something about me that the MEP captain found disagreeable. The disapproval in his eyes was unmistakable.

"Do you have any ideas at all, Mr. Bartlett?"

The girl's cool blue eyes were a relief after the somber brown ones. It was like returning from Milton's *Paradise Lost* to the carefree *L'Allegro* of his youth. Abruptly, the inspiration I'd been searching for materialized—almost at my fingertips.

"Blue eyes," I said. "I'd definitely want her to have blue eyes—and dark brown hair to go with them. And then I'd want her to have a round, full face, and shoulders that look good even in a Mayflower dress."

I saw the telltale pinkness come into her cheeks and I caught the tiny fluttering of a pulse in her white temple. But all she said was: "What else, Mr. Bartlett? I presume she would have intellectual as well as physical qualities."

"Naturally." I knew I was being presumptuous, that I was probably violating some of the law-enforced mores of the Age of Repentance. But for once in my life I felt reckless.

I concentrated on the piquant face before me. "I'd want her to be a little on the sophisticated side," I said softly (the MEP captain had big ears). "Well-versed in the Five Books of course—and perhaps acquainted with one or two of the forbidden ones. And then I'd want her to like children and maybe be willing to have three—or even four—instead of one or none. But most of all I'd want her to be able to freeze any wrong thoughts a man might have about her, not by recourse to the law, or by saying or doing anything; but just by looking the way she does, by being the way she is—if you know what I mean."

The pinkness of her cheeks had darkened to deep rose. "Is that all, Mr. Bartlett?"

I sighed. My recklessness had netted me nothing. "Yes," I said.

She withdrew the application from the talk-typer and initialed it. She raised her eyes. "I censored your reference to the forbidden books," she said. "It would have rated you at least two years in Purgatory if the Marriage Administrator had seen it. You really should be more careful about what you say, Mr. Bartlett."

I'd forgotten all about the meticulous little machine tap-tapping silently away on the desk. I felt like a fool. "Thanks," I said.

"One of the reverend psychiatrists will interview you on the top floor. You'll find a waiting room at the head of the staircase."

I started to turn, then paused. I didn't know why I paused; I only knew that I couldn't let it end like that.

"I wonder," I said.

"Yes?"

"You obtained a lot of information from me but I don't know a single thing about you. Not even your name."

The blue eyes had become arctic lakes. Then, suddenly, they filled with the sparkling warmth of spring. A smile dawned on her lips and her face became a sunrise.

"Julia," she said. "Julia Prentice."

"I'm glad to have known you," I said.

"And I, you, Mr. Bartlett. And now if you'll please excuse me, there are other applicants waiting."

There were—a whole benchful of them. I walked past them glumly, hating them, hating myself, hating a society that would not permit me to choose my own mate; but most of all hating Big Cupid, the mechanized matchmaker that would choose for me.

I paused at the foot of the stone staircase, turned for a final look at Julia. She was interviewing the next applicant. She had forgotten me already.

But someone else in the departmented chamber hadn't. The gaunt MEP captain was more absorbed in me than ever. And, judging from his expression, he no longer merely disapproved of me—he despised me.

Why? Had he overheard my conversation with Julia? I did not think so. With the confused murmur of hundreds of other voices all around him, he could scarcely have singled out mine, especially in view of the fact that I had spoken softly.

But perhaps not softly enough. In any event, he was looking at me as though I were a hopeless habitué of Vanity Fair desperately in need of an Evangelist. I felt like walking over to his desk and asking him the way to the Celestial City. But I didn't. You don't make flippant remarks to MEP officers, particularly when those remarks involve one of the Five Books. You don't, if you want to stay out of Purgatory.

Instead, I turned and started up the stairs to the eyrie of the reverend psychiatrists.

CHAPTER II

It was late afternoon by the time I got out of the Marriage Administration Building. The sun, red and swollen from the spring dust storms, was just disappearing behind the distant elevators of the plankton conversion plant, and the sky was beginning to lose its coppery haze. I hailed a rickshaw, leaned back in the plastic chair and let the June wind cool my face.

The street murmured with the whir of rickshaw wheels and the rhythmic pounding of runners' feet. The Marriage Administration Building faded into the lengthening shadows. The Cathedral drifted grayly by, the tiny windows of its serried chapels glinting red in the final rays of the sun. Then the massive pile of the Coliseum, silent and somber and brooding. In the distance, the hives towered darkly into the sky.

The Coliseum gave way to the parsonage apartments. Prim facades frowned down on me with narrow-windowed righteousness. I shifted uneasily in my rickshaw seat. If my surreptitious reading of the forbidden books had given me a new perspective on the Age of Repentance, it had also given me a troubled conscience.

Just the same, I knew that as soon as the next book "collection" got under way, I would offer my services to the Literature Police just as I'd done a dozen times before. And if my luck held, and I was assigned to sentry duty in the book dump, I would read just as many forbidden volumes as I could every time I got the chance. Moreover, this time I would risk Purgatory and try to save a few of them from the flames.

The parsonage apartments petered out and the noisome market area took their place. Rickshaw traffic densened, competed with hurrying pedestrians. Plastic heels clacked and ankle-length skirts swished in the gloom. The hives occluded the sky now, and the stench of cramped humanity rode the night wind.

I dropped a steel piece into the runner's hand when he pulled up before my hive. I tipped him a plastic quarter when he handed me my change. I could feel the loneliness already, the crushing loneliness that comes to all men who live in faceless crowds.

But I didn't regret having come to the hives to live. They were no lonelier than the YMCA had been. And three rooms, no matter how small, were certainly preferable to the cramped little cubicle I had occupied during the years immediately following my parents' suicide.

A long time ago—a century perhaps, maybe more—the hives bore the more euphemistic name of "apartment houses." But they had corridors then instead of yard-wide passageways, elevators instead of narrow stairways, rooms instead of roomettes. Those were the years before the metal crisis, before the population upsurge; the years that constituted the Age of Wanton Waste.

Deploring the appetites of one's ancestors is a frustrating pastime. I did not indulge in it now. Climbing the four flights of stairs to my apartment, I thought instead of my imminent marriage, hoping to take the edge off my loneliness.

I concentrated on my wife-to-be. A wife, according to the pamphlet that had accompanied my marriage summons, guaranteed to be my ideal mate, emotionally, intellectually, and physically. A wife who would personify my unconscious conception of a goddess, who would fulfill my unconscious standards of feminine beauty, who would administer faithfully to my unconscious emotional needs. In short, just exactly the kind of woman I had unconsciously wanted all my miserable lonely life.

I tried to picture her. I threw everything out of my mind and left my mental retina blank. It did not remain blank for long. Gradually, the twentieth century landscape came into focus—the river flowing in the foreground, bluer than before, the green sea of the meadow spreading out to the exquisite forested hills, the impeccable cumulus mountain, and finally, the solitary bird soaring in the vast sky . . . .

I prepared and ate a frugal meal in the kitchenette, then I shaved, went into the bedroomette and changed into my sentry suit. I was combing my shoulder-length hair when the knock on the door sounded.

I waited, listening for the knock to sound again. I knew practically no one in the city, save the members of my own guard detail, and it was unlikely that any of them would visit me. They saw enough of me on the graveyard shift.

Who, then?

PILGRIMS' PROJECT

The knock sounded again, rising unmistakably above the background noises of the hive—the dull clatter of plastic pots and pans and dishes, the nagging voices of wives, the strident ones of husbands, and the whining of children. I land down my comb, left the bedroomette, stepped across the parlorette, opened the door—and stepped back involuntarily.

The MEP captain had been seated when I had seen him at Marriage Administration Headquarters, and I hadn't been particularly impressed by his size. Standing, he was an arresting sight. The top of his high, wide-brimmed hat touched the ceiling of the passageway; the charcoal coat that hung so loosely on his shoulders could not conceal their striking width; large bony wrists with huge arthritic hands protruded from their cuffs. He looked like a giant who had never had enough to eat.

As I stood staring, he removed his hat and, reaching into an inside pocket of his coat, produced a stained plastic badge. He waved it briefly before my eyes, then replaced it. "Captain Taigue," he said in a voice as thin and unpleasant as his face. "I have a few questions to ask you, Mr. Bartlett."

The shock of finding him on my doorstep had left me numb. But I remembered my rights. "You've no right to ask me questions," I said. "I'm a single man."

"I was invested with the right today when you applied for a wife. A husband-to-be is as securely bound to the laws of matrimony as an actual husband is."

He began to move through the doorway. I either had to get out of the way or be pushed aside. I got out of the way. Taigue shut the door behind him and sat down in the parlorette chair. He fixed me with his brooding eyes.

"Tell me, Mr. Bartlett, do you accept the basic tenets embraced by the marriage amendment?"

I still wasn't sure whether he had jurisdiction over me or not, but I decided to cooperate. I was curious to know the reason for his visit.

"Naturally I accept them," I said.

"Then you devoutly believe that enforced monogamy is the final answer to the deplorable serialized polygamy that characterized the sexual relationships of the twentieth century and brought on the conjugal chaos of the twenty-first; that strict adherence to the monogamous ideal is mandatory if it is to be perpetuated; that the marital unions computed by the Marriage Integrator can never be questioned because they are the ultimate in emotional, physical, and intellectual rapport—"

"I said I accepted the tenets," I said. "What more do you want?"

"That adultery," Taigue went on implacably, "is the most despicable crime a citizen can commit against his society; that adultery has many subtle phases, among the subtlest being the proclivity on the part of some husbands and husbands-to-be to look at women other than their wives or wives-to-be—and lust! You *do* devoutly believe these things, do you not, Mr. Bartlett?"

"Look, Captain," I said. "I spent the whole afternoon being cross-examined by a reverend psychiatrist. He knows more about my sexual nature now than I do myself. If you doubt my marital fitness, why don't you read his report?"

"Psychiatrists are fools," Taigue said. "I investigate applicants in my own way. Now, for the last time, Mr. Bartlett, do you devoutly believe the tenets I have just enumerated?"

"Yes!" I shouted.

"Then why did you look at the girl who took your application this morning—and lust?"

The question staggered me. It betrayed a fantastic overzealousness in his pursuit of his duty—an overzealousness so consuming that it had warped his perspective, had made him see sin where no sin existed. Julia Prentice was one woman whom you could *not* look at and lust. It was that particular quality, I realized now, that had attracted me to her in the first place.

I knew my face was burning; and I knew that Taigue was just the kind of a man who would deliberately interpret a manifestation of anger as a manifestation of guilt if it suited his predilections. The knowledge infuriated me all the more. In his eyes I was guilty, and nothing I could do would prove I wasn't.

I waited until I was sure I could control my voice. Then I said: "I think you've been fasting too long, Captain. Your hallucinations are getting the best of you."

He took no offense. In fact, he smiled as he got slowly to his feet. But his eyes burned with a sort of crazed satisfaction that was either the essence of dedication or the flickering of incipient insanity.

13

"I did not expect you to answer my question, Mr. Bartlett," he said. "I merely wished to apprise you of the alertness of the MEP, and to warn you that any further attention you may bestow on Julia Prentice will not go unobserved—or unpunished."

"You can leave any time," I said, opening the door.

"I can also return any time. Remember that, Mr. Bartlett. And remember the new commandment—*Thou shalt not look at a woman and lust!*"

His tall starved body swayed slightly as he moved through the doorway. It was all I could do to keep my fists at my sides, all I could do to hold back the violent words and phrases that swirled in my mind. When the door swung shut, eclipsing the charcoal shoulders, I collapsed against it.

I had heard tales of the zealots who guarded the matrimonial sanctity of society; I had even visited the Coliseum when a stoning was taking place and seen the battered bloody bodies of the victims lying in the dirt of the arena. But somehow neither the tales nor the bodies had driven home the truth that overwhelmed me now.

When the inevitable metal crisis followed the production-consumption orgy of the late twentieth and early twenty-first centuries and the material world began to fall apart, the people turned to religion for succor. The subsequent merging of the two main churches was a milestone in religious progress. But then the trend went so far that the people elected church officials to represent them and began to stress outward manifestations of virtue by regressing to Puritanical dress and by voluntarily limiting their literary fare to the Bible, *Paradise Lost*, *The Pilgrims' Progress*, *The Scarlet Letter*, and *The Divine Comedy*.

The first clergy-congress was as zealous as the first ordained president in the drafting and the passing of the marriage amendment. And the frugal way of life already adopted by the people was ideal for a world down to its last inch of topsoil. The Marriage Integrator fitted into the new scheme of things nicely, for it justified the stern enforcement of the new marriage laws. And so marriage became a duty rather than a privilege.

I'd been profoundly distrustful of machine-made marriages ever since my parents' suicide, and the surreptitious reading I'd done on the various occasions when I had access to the book dump had increased that distrust.

Marriage, according to all the old literature I'd read on it, was a pretty complex undertaking, so replete with subtleties that it was difficult to imagine a computing machine, no matter how intricate it might be, capable of dealing with them.

There was another aspect about Big Cupid that didn't quite add up. Logically, compatible marriages should result in many children. But most of the married couples in the apartments around me had only one child, and many of them were childless. The condition held true throughout the rest of the city, probably throughout the entire country.

A possible explanation lay in the popular conviction that sex was sin. But it was far from being a satisfactory explanation. The original Puritans identified sex with sin too, but they still raised large families.

No, there was something about Big Cupid that didn't make sense. Moreover, there was something about the Age of Repentance itself that didn't make sense either—when you used books other than the sacred Five for criteria.

The sex orgies which climaxed the Age of Wanton Waste and were influential in bringing about the mass regression to Puritanism, were unquestionably a blot on the scarred escutcheon of civilization. However, they only represented one extreme: the monogamous fanaticism of the Age of Repentance represented the other, which was just as remote from normalcy. Both were wrong.

The society in which I lived and moved was an inconsistent and a rigid society; I had known this for years. But, until now, the knowledge had never bothered me, for I had created the illusion of being a free man by avoiding personal relationships, especially marriage. Now that I could no longer do that, I realized my true status.

I was a prisoner—and Taigue was my keeper.

CHAPTER III

I stood by the yawning mouth of the newly exhumed grave and swore. I had only been on duty two hours, but I had lost a Cadillac-corpse already.

I shifted the beam of my pocket torch from the deep impressions made by the 'copter feet to the tumbled earth around the huge grave mouth, then into the empty grave itself. The gun metal casket had left a neat rectangle in the blue clay when the cargo winch had yanked it loose. Staring down at the smooth, mute subsoil, I felt like Christian wallowing in the Slough of Despond.

I had lied to Julia. Things were not under control at Cadillac. This was the fourth car-corpse I had lost during the past month, and I shuddered when I thought of what the Cadillac Sexton would probably say to me in the morning.

The fact that I'd lost no time in notifying the Air Police was small consolation. The half dozen decrepit 'copters they had at their disposal were no match for the streamlined jobs of the ghouls. The ghouls would get away just as they always did and one more car-corpse would be dismembered and sold on the black market—or contribute its vital steel, copper and aluminum to the clandestine manufacture of newer and swifter 'copters.

I kicked a lump of loose dirt. I felt sick. Around me, tall lombardies formed a palisade so dense that the light of the gibbous moon couldn't penetrate it. Above me, Mars shone like an inflamed red eye. For a moment I wished I were up there, a member of the abandoned colony in *Deucalionis Regio*.

But only for a moment. The ordinary rigors of colonial life were as nothing compared to the rigors that must have faced the Martian colonists when the metal crisis terminated the building of spaceships and brought about the colony's isolation. Perhaps those rigors had eased by now, and then again, perhaps *Deucalionis Regio* had turned into the Valley of the Shadow of Death.

I turned and began walking back to the ganglion tower whence Betz's alarm had summoned me. Betz hailed me when I approached tower 6, and I paused. I could see his round youthful face in the moonlight. The silvery albedo made it seem like a small moon itself as he peered down at me from his eyrie. I had never thought much of him—probably because he had applied

16

for a wife nine years before he needed to and was already a married man. I thought even less of him now.

"I can't understand how they got down without my seeing them," he said.

"I can't understand either," I said.

"It's these damn trees," Betz said. "Some of them are higher than the towers. I don't see how the Sexton expects us to do a good job of guarding when we can't see what we're trying to guard."

"It helps if you keep your eyes open," I said, and walked away.

But whether I liked it or not, his objection was valid. While the Cadillac Cemetery had none of the sprawling vastness of Ford Acres, its decorative landscaping made the deployment of a limited guard detail a difficult proposition. The ancient automakers anticipated neither the future value of their enshrined products nor the sacrilegious exhumings that were to begin a century later, and when they laid out their car cemeteries, they stressed beauty rather than practicality. I could not feel any kindness toward a long dead manufacturer with a penchant for lombardy poplars, weeping willows, and arborvitae; who, seemingly, had done everything in his power to make it easy for twenty-second century ghouls to dig up car-corpses right under sentries' noses and whisk them away in swift cargo 'copters.

As I made my way toward the ganglion tower, I thought of what I would say to the Cadillac Sexton in the morning. I prepared my words carefully, then memorized them so that I could deliver them without faltering: *The time has come for the authorities to decide which is the more important—the scenic beauty of the ground itself, or the security of the sacred corpses beneath the ground. No sentry, however alert he may be, can be expected, to see through trees, and now that the rains are over and the new foliage has reached maximum growth, the situation is crucial and will remain so until fall—*

I went all out. The more responsibility I could foist on the time of the year, the less I would have to assume myself. The Ford Acres Sexton had given me a glowing recommendation when I'd applied for the post at Cadillac several years back, and I hated to lose face in the Cadillac Sexton's eyes. The money was good, much better than at Ford, and with a wife on the way I couldn't afford the cut in salary that relegation to an inferior cemetery would entail.

17

PILGRIMS' PROJECT

Anyway, the time of the year *was* to blame. What other reason could there possibly be for my losing so many car-corpses?

*

But the Cadillac Sexton took a dim view of my suggestion when he showed up the next morning. He glowered at me from behind his desk in the caretaker's office and I could tell from the deepening of the creases in his bulbous forehead that I was in for a lecture.

"Trees are rare enough on Earth as it is without wantonly destroying them," he said, when I had finished talking. "And these particular trees are the rarest of the rare."

He shook his head deploringly. "I'm afraid you don't quite understand the finer points of our mission, Bartlett. The scenic beauty which you would have me devastate is an essential part of the mechanistic beauty, the memory of which we are trying to perpetuate. There is a higher purpose behind the automobile trust funds than the mere preservation of twentieth century vehicles. In setting those funds aside, the ancient automakers were endeavoring to return, symbolically and in a different form, the elements they had taken from the Earth. It was a noble gesture, Bartlett, a very noble gesture, and the fact that we today disapprove of the Age of Wanton Waste does not obviate the fact that the Age of Wanton Waste could—and did—produce art. The symbolic immortality of that art is our responsibility, our mission.

"No, Bartlett, we can never resort to the sacrilegious leveling of trees and shrubbery in an attempt to solve our problem. Its solution lies in greater vigilance on the part of sentries, particularly senior sentries. Our mission is a noble one, one not lightly to be regarded. It behooves us—"

He went on and on in the same vein. After a while, when it became evident that he wasn't going to relegate me to Chevrolet Meadows or Buick Lawn, I relaxed. His idealism was high-flown, but I could endure it as long as the money kept coming in.

When he finally dismissed me, I started back to the hives. I couldn't help thinking, as I walked along the crumbling ancient highway, that if the manufacturers of the late twentieth and early twenty-first centuries had been a little less zealous in their production of art, the Mesabi iron range might be

18

something more than a poignant memory and there might have been enough ore available to have made mass 'copter production something more than an interrupted dream. There was an element of irony in using a super-highway for a footpath.

I hailed a rickshaw at the outskirts of the city and rode in style to my apartment. There was a letter in my mail receptacle. The return address said: MARRIAGE ADMINISTRATION HEADQUARTERS. I waited till I got to my roomettes before I opened it. I wouldn't have opened it then if I'd dared not to.

The message was brief:

> *Report 1500, City Cathedral,*
> *Chapel 14, for marital union*
> *with one Julia Prentice, cit. no.*
> *14489304-P, as per M. I.*
> *directive no. 38572048954-PR.*

I read it again. And again. It still said Julia Prentice.

I knew my heart was beating a lot faster than it normally did and I knew my hands were trembling. I also knew that I was reacting like a fool. There were probably a hundred Julia Prentices in the hive sector alone and probably a hundred more in the other residential districts. So the chance that this Julia Prentice was the one I wanted her to be was one in two hundred.

But my heart kept up its rapid pace and my hands went right on trembling, and I kept seeing that beautiful flowing river with the green sweep of meadow just beyond, the lovely forested hills and the white white cloud; the dark and forlorn speck of the soaring bird . . . .

*

She was there waiting for me, standing in the Cathedral corridor before the little door of Chapel 14, and she was *the* Julia Prentice. I asked myself no questions as to why and wherefore. The reality of her sufficed for the moment.

She looked at me as I came up, then quickly dropped her eyes. The blue polka dots of her new sunbonnet matched her new Priscilla Mullins dress.

19

"I never thought it would be you," I said. "I still can't believe it."

"And why not me?" She would not raise her eyes but kept them focused on the lapel of my John Alden coat. "Why not me as well as someone else? I had a right to apply for a husband. I'm of age. I had nothing to do with the Marriage Integrator's decision."

"I didn't say you did."

"You implied it. I think you are conceited. Furthermore, I think you're being quixotic about a perfectly prosaic occurrence. There's nothing in the least romantic about two pasteboard cards meeting in the digestive system of the Marriage Integrator and finding themselves compatible."

I stared at her. I'd been under the impression, during the brief interval I'd talked with her the preceding day, that she liked me. But perhaps liking a total stranger whom you never expected to see again was different from liking a near total stranger who was very shortly going to be your husband. For the second time during the past twenty-four hours I found myself wallowing in the Slough of Despond.

"I didn't have anything to do with the Marriage Integrator's decision either," I said flatly. I turned away from her and faced the chapel door.

It was a real wooden door, with a stained glass window. The design on the window depicted a stoning in the Coliseum. There were two people standing forlornly in the arena—a man and a woman. They stood with their heads bowed, the scarlet letters on their breasts gleaming vividly. The first stone had just struck the ground at their feet; the second stone hovered in the air some distance away. The encompassing stoning platform was crowded with angry people fighting for access to the regularly spaced stone piles, and high above the scene the Coliseum flag fluttered proudly in the breeze, its big red letter proclaiming that a chastisement was in progress.

There were a dozen other couples waiting in the corridor now, shyly conversing or staring silently at the stained glass windows before them. I wondered if they felt the way I felt, if they had the same misgivings.

The minutes inched by. The silence between Julia and myself became intolerable. I pondered the meaning of the word "compatibility," and wondered why unconscious rapport should manifest itself in conscious hatred.

I remembered my own lonely childhood—the long evenings spent in my parents' hive apartment, the endless dissension between my mother and my father, my father's relegation to the parlorette couch and my mother's key in the bedroomette door, their suicidal leap twenty stories to the street when I was nineteen years old.

I thought of how crowded the hive school had been when I attended it and I wondered suddenly if it was crowded now. I thought of the increasing number of empty apartments in the hive sector, and the cold breath of a long dormant suspicion blew icily through my mind. The world quivered, began to fall apart—

And then Julia said: "I was very rude to you. I didn't mean to be. I'm sorry, Mr. Bartlett."

The world steadied, came back into proper focus. "My name is Roger," I said.

"I'm sorry, Roger."

The marriage chimes began to sound, appending a tinkling ellipsis to her words. I opened the door with trembling fingers and we stepped into the chapel together. The door closed silently behind us.

Before us stood a life-size TV screen. At our elbows, electric candles combined their radiance with the feeble sunlight eking through the narrow stained glass window above the screen and made a half-hearted attempt to chase away the gloom. A basket of synthetic flowers bloomed tiredly at our feet.

Julia's face was pale, but no paler, probably, than mine was. Suddenly sonorous music throbbed out from a concealed speaker and the TV screen came to life. The Marriage Administrator materialized before us, tall, black-garbed, austere of countenance.

He did not speak till the marriage music ended. Then he said: "When I raise my left hand the first time, you will pronounce your own names clearly and distinctly so that they can be recorded in the tape-contract. When I raise my left hand the second time, you will pronounce, with equal clarity and distinctness, the words 'I do.'

"Do you—" He paused and raised his left hand.

"Julia Prentice."

"Roger Bartlett."

"Take this man-woman to be your lawful wedded husband-wife?" He raised his left hand again.

"I do." We spoke the words together.

"Then by the power invested in me by the marriage amendment, I pronounce you man and wife and sentence you to matrimony for the rest of your natural lives."

CHAPTER IV

It was some time before I remembered to kiss my bride. When I did remember, the twentieth century landscape spread out around me and I had the distinct impression that the world had stirred beneath my feet, had hesitated, for a fraction of a second, on its gargantuan journey around the sun.

The voice of the Marriage Administrator was deafening, his face purple. "There will be no osculating in the chapels! The chapels will be cleared immediately for the next applicants. There will be no—"

Neither of us had known that the screen was a transmitter as well as a receiver, and we moved apart guiltily. A shower of plastic rice poured down on us as we stepped through the doorway. We ran laughing down the corridor, picked up our marriage contract at the vestibule window, and stepped out into the Cathedral court.

The afternoon sun was bright in the coppery sky but the shadow of the pulpit platform lay cool and dark across the eastern flagstones. We walked across the congregation area to the vaulted entrance that led to the street. I hailed a double rickshaw and we rode to the YWCA and picked up Julia's things. Then we headed for the hives.

I'd called in the converters, of course. They'd done their work rapidly and well. I noticed the changes the moment I opened the door.

There were two chairs in the parlorette now, both smaller than the old one had been, but charming in their identical design. A table had replaced the tableette in the kitchenette and an extra stool now stood by the enlarged cupboard. Through the bed-roomette doorway I could see one of the corners of the new double bed.

I stepped into the parlorette, waited for Julia to follow me. When she did not, I returned to the passageway. She was standing there quietly, her eyes downcast, her hands folded at the waist of her new blue dress. It struck me abruptly that she was the most beautiful thing I had ever seen and simultaneously it dawned on me why she hadn't followed me in.

The custom was so old—so absurd. It was almost a part of folklore, a tattered remnant of the early years of the twentieth century when newlyweds had tried to insure by fetish the conjugal permanence that was now enforced by law.

And yet, in a way, it was beautiful.

I stood for a moment, memorizing Julia's pale fresh loveliness. Then I lifted her into my arms and carried her across the threshold.

*

Guarding interred Cadillacs was far from being an ideal way to spend my wedding night, but after the way things had been going I hadn't dared to ask the Sexton for an extra night off. I donned my sentry suit in the darkness, moving quietly so as not to awaken Julia, then I descended to the street and hailed a rickshaw. It was past 2300 and I had to ride all the way to the cemetery in order to get there on time.

After posting the other sentries, I relieved the 1600-2400 senior sentry in the ganglion tower. He had nothing of interest to report and I sent him on his way. Standing beneath the big rotating searchlight, watching him descend the ladder, I envied him his night's freedom.

The searchlight threw a moving swath of radiance over artificial hill and dale, shone like an ephemeral sun on arborvitae patterns, blazed on the green curtains of lombardy stands. I cursed those noncommittal curtains for the thousandth time, deplored my inability to do anything about them.

The size of the cemetery precluded any practical patrol of the grounds. All I could do was hope that I, or one of the other sentries in the strategically located towers, would spot any unusual movement, hear any unusual sound.

I touched the cold barrel of the tower blaster. My fingers were eager for the feel of the trigger, my eyes hungry for the spiderweb of the sight. I had never brought down a ghoul 'copter—for the simple reason that I had never had a good shot at one. But I was looking forward to the experience.

It was a cool night for June. The wind had shifted to the northeast, washing the haze of the western dust storms from the atmosphere, and the stars stood out, bold and clear. Mars was no longer an inflamed red eye but a glowing pinpoint of pure orange. *Deucalionis Regio*, however, was as much of an enigma as ever.

An hour passed. The sentries phoned in their reports and I recorded them on the blotter.

0100—all quiet on the Cadillac Front.

My thoughts shifted to Julia, and the magic of the night deepened around me. I pictured her sleeping, her hair dark against the pillow, the delicate crescents of her lashes accentuating the whiteness of her cheeks; her supple body curved in relaxed grace beneath the sheets. I listened to the soft sound of her breathing—

Soft? No, not soft. My Julia breathed loudly. Moreover, she breathed with a regularity hard to associate with a human being—a regularity reminiscent of a machine. Specifically, a malfunctioning machine, and more specifically yet, the turning of a borer shaft in a well-oiled, but worn, sleeve.

Alert now, I tried to locate the sound. At first it seemed to be all around me, a part of the night air itself, but I finally narrowed it down to the northeast section of the cemetery. Tower 11's territory.

I called 11. Kester's lean young face came into focus on the telescreen. "You should be hearing a borer," I said. "Unless you're deaf. *Do* you hear one?" Kester's face seemed strained. "Yes. I—I think so."

"Then why didn't you report it? I can hear the damn thing way over here!"

"I—I was going to," Kester said. "I wanted to make sure."

"Make sure! How sure do you have to be? Now listen. You stay by your blaster and keep your eyes and your ears open. I'm coming over to see if I can locate the 'copter. If I do locate it I'll throw a flare under it, and if they try to rise, you burn them. If they don't try to rise and we can take them alive, so much the better. I'd like to see a real live ghoul. But otherwise, you burn them! If we lose another car-corpse, we'll all be out on Our ears."

"All right," Kester said. The screen went blank.

Descending the tower ladder, I wondered what kind of a guard detail I had. Last night, Betz's negligence had cost me a Cadillac. Tonight, Kester's negligence had very nearly cost me another—and might yet, if I wasn't careful.

I couldn't understand it. They were both newly-married men (Kester had applied for a wife the same day Betz had) and, since women were forbidden to work after marrying, both of them certainly needed the better wages Cadillac paid. Why should they deliberately jeopardize their status?

PILGRIMS' PROJECT

Maybe Betz really hadn't seen or heard anything until it was too late. Maybe Kester really hadn't been sure that the sound he was hearing was the turning of a borer.

But I was sure, and the closer I got to Tower 11, the surer I became. I timed my approach with the swath of the searchlight, made certain there was plenty of concealment available whenever it passed my way. That wasn't hard to do, with all the lombardies, the arborvitae, the hills, dales and gardens that infested the place. But for once the ancient automakers' passion for landscaping was benefitting me instead of the ghouls.

Tower 11 was a tripodal skeleton stabbing into the cadaverous face of the rising moon. It loomed higher and higher above me as I neared the source of the sound. I swore silently at Kester. He was either stone deaf and blind as a bat, or a deliberate traitor to the Cadillac cause. The exhuming was taking place practically under his nose.

I crept beneath the hem of a lombardy curtain and lay in the deep shadows. I could see the cargo 'copter clearly now. It squatted over a grave mound less than twenty feet from my hiding place, its rotating borer protruding from its open belly like an enormous stinger. The grave mound was already perforated with a score of holes, spaced so that when the car-casket was drawn upward, the hard-packed earth would crumble and fall apart.

The borer was now probing for the eye of the casket. Even as I watched I heard the grind of steel against gun metal, saw the borer reverse its spiral and rise swiftly into the hold of the 'copter. A bright light stabbed down into the new hole, was quickly extinguished. I thought I heard the sound of a breath being expelled in relief, but I wasn't sure. Shortly thereafter, I heard the almost inaudible hum of a winch motor, saw the hook dangling on the end of the steel cable just before it disappeared into the hole.

I pulled a flare from my belt, broke the seal. My aim was excellent. The flare landed in the center of the grave mound, went off the minute it hit the ground. The light was blinding. The whole northeast section of the cemetery became as bright as noonday, the interior of the 'copter leaped into dazzling detail. I could see the dungaree-clad ghouls standing on the edge of the open hatch. I could see the winch operator's face—

It was a striking face. It was a twentieth century landscape. The smear of grease on one of the pink cheeks had no effect whatsoever on the white cloud. The blue eyes, blinded by the unexpected light, flowed their blue and beautiful way along the green lip of the nonpareil meadow. The forested hills were more exquisite than ever—

But the solitary bird was gone, and the sky was empty.

And then, suddenly, I could not see anything at all. The ground erupted as the casket broke free, and a shower of dirt and broken clods engulfed me. I staggered to my feet, shielding my eyes with my arms, gasping for breath. By the time I regained my vision the copter was high above the lombardies, the exhumed car-casket swinging wildly beneath the still-opened hatch.

Don't shoot! my mind screamed to Kester. *Don't shoot!* But the words were locked in my throat and I could not utter them. I could only stand there helplessly, waiting for the disintegrating beam to lance out from the tower, waiting for the 'copter and the ghouls—and my conniving Julia—to become bright embers in the night sky.

But I needn't have worried. Kester missed by a mile.

*

I turned him in. What else could I do? I'd spent nine years languishing in lonely towers through long and lonely nights, faithfully guarding the buried art of the automakers. I couldn't throw those years away out of foolish loyalty to a man as obviously indifferent to the cause as Kester was.

But I didn't feel very proud of myself, standing there in the Cadillac Sexton's office the next morning, with Kester, his face cold and expressionless, standing beside me. I didn't feel proud at all. And the Sexton's praise of my last night's action only turned my stomach.

I was cheating and I knew it. I should have turned in Julia too. But I couldn't do that. Before I took any action, I had to see her, question her myself. There had to be a reasonable explanation for her complicity. There *had* to be!

After the Sexton dismissed me I waited outside for Kester. He didn't seem like a chastened man when he stepped into the morning sunlight. If anything, he seemed relieved—if not actually happy.

He would have walked right by me without a word, but I touched his shoulder and he paused. "I'm sorry," I said. "I didn't want to turn you in but I had no choice. But the Sexton let you go?"

He nodded.

"I'm sorry," I said again.

He looked at me for a long moment. Then he said: "Bartlett, you're a fool," and turned and walked away.

CHAPTER V

Julia wasn't in the apartment when I got home. But Taigue was.

He was sitting in one of the new chairs as though he owned the place. This time he hadn't come alone. The other chair was occupied by an MEP patrolman armed with a bludgeon gun.

"Come in," Taigue said. "We've been expecting you."

I don't know why I should have cared after the events of last night, but the thought of what he might have done to Julia crystallized my blood. "Where's Julia?" I said.

"Why, what a unique coincidence, Mr. Bartlett. Truly, our minds run in the same channel, to coin a cliché. I was about to voice the same plaintive question."

He was still fasting, and the increased gauntness of his face accentuated the fanatical intensity of his eyes. "If you've hurt her," I said, "I'll kill you!"

Taigue's ugly, dolichocephalic head swivelled on his thin neck till he faced his assistant. "Look who's going to kill someone, Officer Minch. Our esteemed candidate for the Letter himself!"

That one set me back on my heels. I felt the strength go out of my legs. "You're out of your mind, Captain. I'm legally married and you know it!"

"Indeed, Mr. Bartlett?" He reached into the inside pocket of his coat, withdrew a folded sheet of synthetic paper. He tossed it to me contemptuously. "Read all about your 'marriage,' Mr. Bartlett. Then tell me if I'm out of my mind."

I unfolded the gray document, knowing what it was and yet refusing to accept the knowledge. All warrants for arrest are unpleasant to the recipient, but an MEP warrant is triply unpleasant.

In addition to being a warrant, it is an indictment, and in addition to being an indictment, it is a sentence. A marital offender has automatically waived his right to a trial of any kind by the very nature of his offense. The logic of the first Puritanical legislators was muddied by their unnatural horror of illicit sex—an inevitable consequence of their eagerness to atone for the sexual enormities of their forebears.

PILGRIMS' PROJECT

I read the words, first with disbelief, then, as the realization of Julia's motivation dawned on me, with nausea:

> CHARGE: *Adultery, as per paragraph 34 of the Adultery Statute, which states in effect that all unofficial marital relationships, regardless of potential ameliorating factors, be construed as asocial and classified as adulterous acts.*
> CORRESPONDENTS: *Roger Bartlett, cit. no. 14479201-B; Julia Prentice, cit. no. 1448-9304-P.*
> PARTICULARS: *M. I. check, suggested and carried out by MEP Captain Lawrence Taigue, disclosed discrepancy in compatibility factors of aforementioned correspondents. Further check revealed deliberate altering of data cards before M. I. computation, rendering said computation invalid and resultant 'marriage' unofficial and therefore adulterous.*
> SENTENCE: *Public chastisement in the arena of the Municipal Coliseum.*
> DATE OF CHASTISEMENT: *June 20, 2151.*
> AUTHORIZED ARRESTING OFFICERS: MEP *Captain Lawrence Taigue; MEP Patrolman Ebenezer Minch.*
> *(signed) Myles Fletcher*
> MARRIAGE ADMINISTRATOR *June 8, 2151*

"Well, Mr. Bartlett? Must you read the words off the page to get their import?"

My mind was reeling but it still rebelled against the reality of Julia's guilt. I grabbed at the first alternative I could think of. "*You* changed the cards, didn't you, Taigue?" I said.

"Don't be ridiculous. The mere thought of bringing an oafish clod like yourself into even transient intimacy with a sublime creature like Julia revolts my finer sensibilities. Julia altered the cards—as you perfectly well know. But she did not alter them of her own free will. You forced her to alter them."

I stared at him. "For God's sake, Captain, use your head! Why should I do such a thing? How—"

"*Why?*" Taigue had risen to his feet. His eyes were dilated. He breathed with difficulty. "I'll tell you why! Because you're a filthy animal, that's why. Because you looked at an ethereal woman and saw nothing but flesh. Because your carnal appetite was whetted and your lecherous desires had to be fed at any cost.

"But you're not going to get away with it!" He was shouting now and his trembling fingers were inches from my throat. "I myself will cast the first stone. But before I do, you'll confess. When the Hour is near, you'll realize the enormity of your lust, just as they all do, and you'll fall on your knees and ask forgiveness. And when you do, you'll automatically absolve Julia of all guilt. *All* guilt, do you understand, Bartlett? Julia's purity must be restored. Julia's purity *has* to be restored!"

I brought my right fist up into his stomach then. Hard. I had to. In another second those yearning fingers would have clamped around my throat.

But I forgot about Patrolman Minch and his bludgeon gun. Even before Taigue hit the floor, the first charge struck me in the shoulder, spun me around so that I faced the wall. The next one caught me squarely in the back of the neck, turned my whole body numb. I sagged like a cloth doll. The floor fascinated me. It was like a dark cloud, rising. A dark cloud, and then a swirling mist of blackness. And then—nothing.

*

Prison cells are ideal for objective thinking. There is a quality about their drab walls that brings you face to face with reality.

The Coliseum cell in which I was confined possessed the ultimate in drab walls. The reality with which I was faced was the ultimate in unpleasantness . . . .

On our wedding night, Julia had told me that she had worked at Marriage Administration Headquarters for three years. But when I mentioned Taigue's concern over her, she was amazed. She said she hardly even knew him, that he had never spoken a word to her, had never—to her knowledge—even looked at her.

But he had looked at her without her knowledge. Of that I was sure. He had looked at her a hundred, a thousand, a million times. He had sat at his desk for three years, admiring her, adoring her, worshiping her.

Beyond her physical appearance, however, his Julia bore no relation to the real Julia. His Julia was far more than an ordinary woman. She was the exquisite vase into which he had thrust the flowers of his idealism.

The celibacy vows he had taken when he was ordained an MEP officer were only partly responsible for his attitude. The real key lay in his physical ugliness—an ugliness that had probably influenced his decision to become an MEP officer.

He had never spoken to Julia, or looked at her openly, because of a deep conviction that he would repel her; and he had rationalized his reticence by attributing it to his rigid interpretation of his duty as an MEP officer. The only way he could realize his love for her was by elevating that love to a higher plane. This had necessitated his elevating Julia also.

Taigue loathed sex. He could tolerate it only when it came as a result of a society-sanctioned marriage. With respect to Julia, he could not tolerate it at all, because the intrusion of sex upon his exquisite vase of flowers sullied both flowers and vase.

When he discovered that the Marriage Integrator had matched Julia with an ordinary mortal, he could not accept the validity of the computation; neither could he accept the fact that Julia had applied for a husband. He had to find a loophole somewhere, a means to rationalize the danger to his flowers. When he learned that Julia herself had contrived the computation, he immediately transferred the blame to me, thereby absolving Julia.

But his logic was shaky, and he knew it. He couldn't quite believe the lies he had told himself. His edifice was tottering and he needed my confession to shore it up. Therein lay my only hope.

For Taigue would buy that confession at any price. And I would sell it for only one price—

My life.

And so I sat there in my lonely cell, through the gray daytime hours and through the dark nights, waiting for Taigue.

I thought often of Julia. In spite of myself I thought of her, and in spite of myself I kept hoping that she would continue to elude the country-wide search which Marriage Enforcement Headquarters had instigated the morning of my arrest.

I thought of her not as Taigue's vase of flowers, but as the pale girl who had said "I do" with me at the mass-wedding ceremony; as the lovely girl who had lingered in the hive passageway, waiting for me to carry her across the threshold; as the unforgettable girl who had been my wife for a dozen precious hours.

But most of all, I thought of her as the deceitful woman who had intended to use me as an instrument in the ghouls' exploitation of the Cadillac Cemetery.

As she had used Betz and Kester before me.

I had her whole *modus operandi* figured out. Her system was simple. When a cemetery sentry applied for a wife, she simply notified an available sister-ghoul, entered her application along with the sentry's, and then altered the resultant data cards so that they came out of the integrator in the right combination. It took a lot of know-how, but she hadn't worked at Marriage Administration Headquarters three years for nothing. She hadn't taken the job in the first place for nothing, either.

Being a senior sentry, I had rated her personal supervision. I had no idea as to what wiles she would have employed to make me voluntarily neglect my duty to Cadillac; but I had an uncomfortable suspicion that they would have worked.

*

Taigue didn't come until the last day—the last hour, in fact. I was sweating. The Coliseum seamstress had already sewn the big scarlet letter on the breast of my gray prison blouse and the Coliseum barber had just been in to cut my hair. I could hear the distant shuffling of feet on the stoning platform and the faraway murmur of many voices.

Taigue was still fasting. Ordinary MEP officers were usually content to fast their required day per week and to let it go at that. But Taigue was not an ordinary MEP officer. He stood before me like a Bunyanesque caricature. Caverns had appeared above the ridges of his cheek bones and his eyes had retreated into their depths where they burned like banked fires.

"Short hair becomes you, Mr. Bartlett," he said, but his irony lacked its usual edge. Moreover, the ghastly paleness of his face could not be wholly attributed to his physical condition.

"Did you come to receive my confession, Captain?"

"Whenever you're ready, Mr. Bartlett."

"I'm ready now."

He nodded solemnly. "I thought you might be. I discounted Julia's insistence that she acted of her own free will."

That shook me. "Julia? Is—is she here?"

He nodded again. "She gave herself up a week ago. She confessed to altering the data cards—insisted over and over that she alone was to blame. I tried to tell them, I tried to explain to the Marriage Administrator that she couldn't possibly be to blame, that she was an innocent tool in the hands of a hardened adulterer. But he wouldn't listen. No one would listen. They sewed the letter on her this morning. They—they cut her hair."

I tried to tell myself that she had it coming, but it wasn't any good. I felt sick. I kept seeing her crumpled body lying in the arena and the cruel stones scattered in the dirt and the blood on them. Julia's blood—

"Well, Mr. Bartlett? You said you were ready to confess."

"Yes," I said. "I presume you're ready to pay my price?"

"Price?" The emaciated face showed surprise. "Do you expect to be reimbursed for relieving your conscience, Mr. Bartlett?"

"You can put it that way if it makes it easier for you."

"And what do you think your confession is worth?"

"You know how much it's worth, Taigue. It's worth Julia's life—and mine."

"You try my patience, Mr. Bartlett."

"You try mine too."

"My wanting your confession is a purely personal matter. Both you and Julia will die in the arena regardless of your decision. Adultery charges are irrevocable."

"I'm not asking you to revoke any charges," I said. "All I'm asking you to do is to get Julia and me out of here alive. You can do it."

He stared at me. "Mr. Bartlett, your incarceration has affected your mind! Do you really think I'd free you, even if I could, and give you further opportunity to vitiate Julia?"

My thinking hadn't been nearly as objective as I'd imagined. I should have realized that Taigue would rather see his flowers dead than expose them to additional "defilement." I was desperate now, and my desperation got the better of my judgment. "Is my confession worth Julia's life then?" I asked.

He raised an arthritic hand to his forehead, wiped away a glistening film of sweat. Presently: "Mr. Bartlett, I'm afraid you don't understand the situation at all. Your perspective is so warped by wrong thinking that 2 and 2 fail to make 4 to you, either by multiplication or addition.

"Don't you see that Julia *has* to die? Can't you understand that, even though she is innocent, her reputation is still hopelessly tainted by your illicit affections? Can't you realize that I wouldn't save her even if I could?"

I did realize finally, though his fanaticism stunned me. He was more than a mere zealot; he was a monster. But if Julia was his goddess, marriage enforcement was his god. He could not buy a guarantee of his goddess' purity if the price involved the desecration of his god. He needed my confession desperately, but he didn't have the authority to torture it out of me and he couldn't pay the price I had asked. My one hope of escape had turned out to be a pretty worthless item.

But it was still my only hope. If I could find another way to use it, it might still net me my freedom, and Julia's too.

There was one way. It was drastic and it might not work; but it was worth a try. "All right, Taigue," I said. "I understand your position. Bring Julia here and I'll confess."

"Bring her here? Why? All you have to do is admit you coerced her to alter the data cards. Her presence isn't necessary."

"It's necessary to me."

He looked at me for a moment, then turned abruptly and left the cell. He told the patrolman, whom he had posted by the door, to wait, then he disappeared down the corridor. The patrolman closed the cell door but didn't bother to lock it. He didn't need to. The bludgeon gun in the crook of his arm was a sufficient deterrent.

Presently I heard Taigue's returning footsteps. They were accompanied by other footsteps —light, quick footsteps. My heart broke the barrier I had erected around it, rose up, choking me.

PILGRIMS' PROJECT

When I saw her shorn hair I wanted to cry. Her face was more like a little girl's than ever, but the blue eyes gazing straight into mine were the eyes of a mature woman. There was regret in them, but no shame.

I turned away from her. "Dismiss your assistant," I told Taigue. "What I have to say is none of his business."

Taigue started to object, then changed his mind. With the reassurance he so desperately needed at his very fingertips, he wasn't in the mood to argue over trivialities. He took the patrolman's bludgeon gun, sent him on his way, re entered the cell and dosed the door. He leaned against the genuine steel panels, directed the muzzle of the gun at my chest.

"Well, Mr. Bartlett?"

"You asked for this, Taigue," I said. "You wouldn't have it any other way. Julia, come here." She stepped to my side. Seizing the lapels of her Hester Prynne prison dress, I ripped it down the middle and tore it from her body.

CHAPTER VI

Julia shrank back, trying to cover her nakedness with her arms. Taigue became a statue, a statue staring with horrified eyes at a shining goddess who had abruptly deteriorated into a mere woman. I tore the gun from his grasp before he could recover himself and bludgeoned him beneath the heart. But his eyes were glazed even before the charge struck him. I looked at him disgustedly as he sank gasping to the floor. The self-righteous idealism with which he had clothed Julia had been even thinner than the earthly clothes I had ripped away.

I turned to Julia. She had retrieved the prison dress, had slipped into it, and was improvising a catch to hold it together. Her face was white but her eyes were dry. I searched those eyes anxiously. I don't know why I should have been relieved to find understanding rather than anger in them, but I was relieved—more relieved than I would have cared to admit.

"Can you pilot a 'copter?" I asked.

She nodded. "I've been piloting them since I was twelve."

"There's a 'copter port on the roof. If we can reach it, we've got a chance. I don't know where we'll go, but we'll go somewhere—"

"We'll go to Mars, Roger. If you're willing." She had finished repairing her dress and stood calm and poised before me.

"This is no time for jokes," I said.

"And I'm not joking. There's a ramp not far from here that will take us to the roof. Come on, Roger!"

We peered up and down the corridor. It was empty. I followed Julia down the grim passage.

In the distance, the arena entrance was bright with afternoon sunlight. At the first intersection, she turned right. The new passage was narrow, dimly lighted. At its far end a ponderous stone door opened reluctantly to the pressure of our shoulders and we found ourselves at the base of a sharply slanting ramp.

"You seem to know this place like a book," I said. "Were you ever in the cell block before?" She nodded. "I visited my mother often before she was stoned."

37

"Your mother! *Stoned?*"

"Yes. Stoned. That's why I'm a ghoul. Hurry, Roger!"

We started up the ramp. After a dozen yards, it turned abruptly, became a steep spiral. Breathing was difficult, conversation impossible. Now and then, a slit of a window looked out into the crowded amphitheater.

The port boasted one derelict 'copter and one guard. The guard had his back to us when we crept cautiously onto the roof. He must have sensed our presence, for he turned. But I doubt if he ever saw us. The charge from my gun struck him in the side before he even completed his turn, and he crumpled to the sun-drenched concrete.

We were aboard the 'copter in an instant. Julia's experienced fingers made deft maneuvers on the control panel and then we were aloft, soaring over the amphitheater, the sky blue above us, the stoning platform a chiaroscuro of gray- and black-garbed men and women below us. The arena proper was a bleak expanse of packed dirt, unrelieved by a single blade of grass. I could hear the obscene murmur of the crowd above the whirring of the blades.

There was a telescreen above the control panel. I turned it on to see if our escape had been discovered. Apparently it had not been, for the scene coming over the single channel was the same I had just witnessed, viewed from a different angle. The telecamera had been set up opposite the arena entrance so that the upper echelon members of the hierarchy, who could afford such luxuries as TV sets, would have an excellent view of the expected chastisement.

The announcer was intoning the sixth commandment over and over in a deep resonant voice. I lowered the volume and turned to Julia. We were over the parsonage apartments now, headed in a northerly direction.

"Don't you think it's time you told me where we're going?" I said.

"I told you before but you wouldn't believe me. We're going to Mars, provided you're willing, of course. And I'm afraid you haven't much choice."

"Stop being ridiculous, Julia. This is a serious situation!"

"I know, darling. I know. And if the ship has already blasted, it will be a far more serious situation."

"What ship are you talking about?"

"The Cadillac-ship; the Ford-ship; the Plymouth-ship. Call it what you will. Cars are made of metal, so are spaceships. By applying the right temperatures, and the right techniques, dedicated people can transform Cadillacs and Fords and Plymouths into highways to the stars."

I was staring at her. "The ghouls—"

"Are people like myself—the new Pilgrims, if you like. Pilgrims sick of a society that evades population control by consigning its marriages to a computer deliberately designed to produce incompatible unions that will result in few, if any, children. Pilgrims who want no more of a civilization victimized by an outdated biblical exhortation, exploited by false prophets hiding behind misinterpretations of Freudian terminology."

The hives were flickering beneath us, gaunt precipices flanking narrow canyons. The verdure of the Cadillac Cemetery showed in the distance, and beyond it, eroded hills rolled away.

"I'm glad you did alter our data cards," I said after a while. "But I wish you'd done it for a different reason. I wish you could have loved me, Julia."

"I do love you," Julia said. "You see, darling, I couldn't accompany the colonists without a husband and I didn't want the kind of a husband the integrator would have given me. So I computed my own marriage. That was why I was so rude to you at the Cathedral. I—I was ashamed. Not that it was the first marriage I'd computed, but all the others—like Betz's and Kester's—involved people who were working on the ship, people who were already in love. There—there wasn't anyone in the group whom I cared for myself, so I had to look elsewhere. You and I are ideally suited, Roger. I didn't need the data cards to tell me that—all I needed was my eyes."

We were high above the Cadillac Cemetery and she was looking anxiously ahead at the rolling, dun-colored hills. "If only they haven't left yet," she said. "The last Cadillac we exhumed provided enough metal to finish the ship. But perhaps they waited for us."

A sudden crescendo in the murmur of the waiting crowd in the Coliseum brought the TV unit back to life. Slowly, the murmur rose into a great vindictive roar. Glancing at the screen, I saw the reason why.

The charcoal-uniformed figure that had just stepped through the arena entrance was unmistakable. The distance was considerable, and the eyes appeared only as dark shadows on the thin, haunted face. But I could visualize the terrible guilt burning in their depths; the consuming, the unbearable guilt—

I watched the first stone with horror. It missed, rolled to a stop in the dirt. The next one missed, too. But the one after it didn't, nor the one that followed. Taigue sank to his knees, and the stones became a murderous hail. And then, abruptly, it was all over, and Taigue lay dead and bleeding on the stone-littered ground, the scarlet letter he had pinned to his breast vivid in the merciless sunlight.

Thou shalt not look at a woman and lust—

Taigue had kept faith with himself to the end.

*

We were drifting over the hills. "There," Julia said suddenly. "There's the one, Roger!" It looked like all the others to me—drab, scarred by innumerable gullies, lifeless. But when Julia opened the door of the cockpit and leaned out and waved, the gullies rivened, and the whole hill opened up like an enormous metallic flower.

I saw the ship then, the tall burnished ship poised on its concrete launching platform. I saw its name—the *Mayflower II.*

We drifted down past the tapered prow, the gleaming flanks. The other Pilgrims were already aboard. Betz and Kester waved to us as we passed the open lock. We stepped out upon the launching platform. The ship towered above us. The lathes and presses and furnaces of the subterranean factory stood silent in the gloom around us.

I looked at Julia. Her eyes were iridescent with relieved tears, her smile tremulous with happiness. "Mars, Roger," she whispered. "The ship can make it. But perhaps the old colony has perished and we'll have to start a new one. It won't be easy, darling. But will you come?"

I felt the way Samuel Fuller and Christopher Martin must have felt five centuries ago, standing on a lonely wharf in Southampton. The way William White and John Alden must have felt—

No, not quite the way John. Alden had felt. I already had *my* Priscilla Mullins. I bent and kissed her. Then, hand in hand, we ascended the spiral gangplank of the *Mayflower II* to begin our journey to the New World.